The Day That Diamond Got STUCK in a Hole

Diamond's Adventures Series

By Jeanna Little

Illustrated By Malic Anila

Written By Jeanna Little

Illustrated By Malic Anila

ISBN Paperback 978-0-578-92584-4

ISBN Hardcover 978-0-578-93263-7

First edition 2021

Dedicated to the sweetest, most loving dog there ever was, Diamond Rio Wyne. I miss you more than words can express. You were the best furry little friend. May your memory live on in the hearts of children forever.

Diamond has BIG plans on this sunny day in Happy Hollow. She wants to play tag with one of her friends down by the pond.

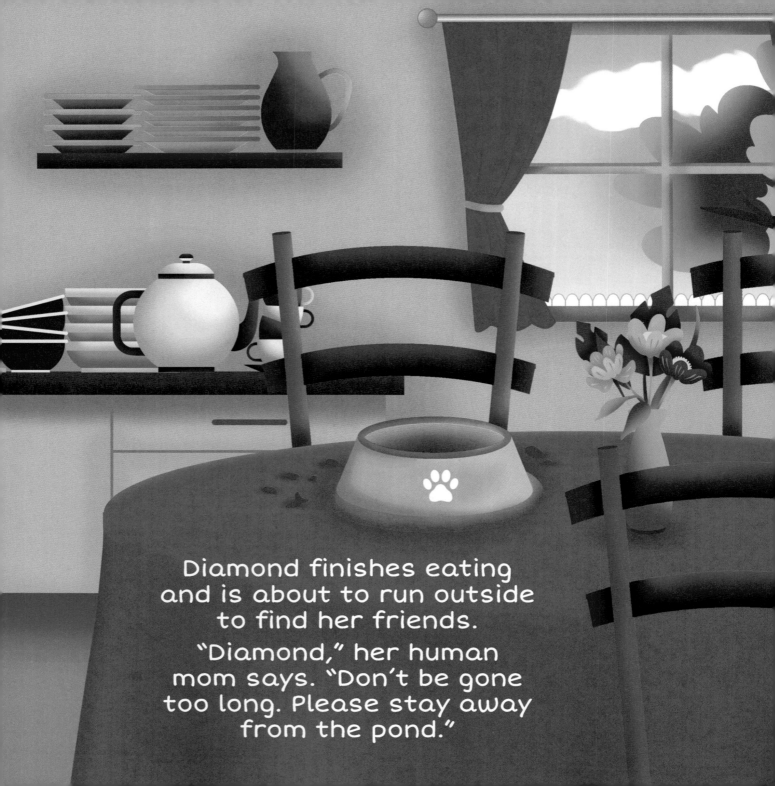

Diamond finishes eating and is about to run outside to find her friends.

"Diamond," her human mom says. "Don't be gone too long. Please stay away from the pond."

Tilly, Thump, and Mr. Bunny live close by. Tilly and Thump are her best friends. Diamond likes Mr. Bunny, but he can be a bit grumpy.

"Hey, Mr. Bunny. How are you? I'm here to see Tilly and Thump," Diamond says, wagging her tail.

"They're finishing their chores while I tend to my garden," Mr. Bunny replies. "Scurry along now so I can get back to it."

"I hope they'll be done soon," Diamond says. Then she shouts, "Tag! You're it!" She speeds off into the woods.

Mr. Bunny smiles and chases after her. "I'm going to get you!"

Diamond zooms in and out of the trees, trying to throw Mr. Bunny off her trail. When she gets near the pond, she is surprised that Mr. Bunny is right behind her.

She leaps high into the air and jumps right in the middle of the biggest puddle. Mud splashes everywhere!

The ground shakes and a deep hole opens beneath her! "Help! Help! Mr. Bunny!" she shouts.

Mr. Bunny hops over to Diamond and finds her stuck in the hole.

"Oh, Diamond. What will we do now?" Mr. Bunny shakes his head. "I'll get help."

Diamond whimpers. "Don't leave me, please. There could be monsters down here!"

"It will be okay," Mr. Bunny shouts down. "I'll get Tilly and Thump to help. I'll be back before you know it!"

Diamond trembles. "Why didn't I listen to my mom?"

Diamond is startled when she hears something behind her. It sounds big and scary! Diamond slowly turns and shrieks.

A tiny earthworm stares back at Diamond.
"You scared me, little guy." Diamond giggles.
"But I'm glad to have some company in
this scary hole."

After what seems like hours, Diamond
hears the hops of little bunny feet.
Friendly faces peer down at her.

"Tilly! Thump! Mr. Bunny!" Diamond shouts.
"I'm so happy to see you!"

"Grab hold of this branch. We'll pull you up!" Tilly squeaks.

Diamond bites down on the end of the branch, waving goodbye to her worm friend.

Mr. Bunny, Tilly, and Thump easily pull her free.

Diamond spins around in circles. "I'm saved!"

Diamond hugs her friends. "Thank you so much! I have to get home and hug my mom."

Diamond looks up slowly
with her puppy dog eyes
and licks her mom's cheek.
"Ruff! Ruff!"

"You've been near the pond, haven't you?" her mom asks.

Diamond burrows her head under her mom's chin, hoping she will forgive her.

Diamond's mom squeezes her tightly. "It's okay, sweet girl. But please be careful. I want to keep you safe because I care about you."

Diamond feels loved in her mom's arms.
She now understands how important it
is to follow the rules.

Diamond plops down on her dog bed for a much-needed nap. Before falling asleep, she thinks about all the things she will get up to tomorrow!

The End

Made in the USA
Columbia, SC
09 November 2022

70754316R00020